here once was a boy called Jack who lived with his mother in a cottage. His father had been dead for some years, and Jack and his mother were very poor. They had sold everything they owned, aside from an old cow.

One morning Jack's mother said, 'The cow's milk has dried up. We have no milk to drink and we can no longer make butter for our bread. You will have to take her to market. Make sure you get a good price.'

Jack did as his mother told him and set off to market. It was a long way to town and Jack was not fond of walking, so after a while he sat down to rest.

As he was nodding off, an old man wandered past.

'Good morning,' he said to Jack. 'That's a bony old cow you have there.'

'I'm taking her to market to sell, even though she is the only thing we have left.'

'No need to go all the way to market,' said the old man. 'I have some magic beans, and I will give them to you in return for your bony old cow.'

'What use are beans?' said Jack. 'Besides, there are only five of them. Our cow is worth more than that.'

'These are magic beans. Take them home and plant them. You won't be disappointed.'

Jack didn't much fancy the long walk to town, so he exchanged the cow for the old man's beans and went home again.

When he got there, with neither cow nor money, his mother scolded and wept. 'What have you done? The cow might have been bony and old, but she was worth more than five beans. You are a hopeless, worthless, good-for-nothing boy!' And with that she hurled the beans out of the window. Then she sent Jack to bed without any supper.

The next morning, Jack awoke to find his room bathed in a strange green light. He looked out of the window, but all he could see was a mass of huge green leaves.

When he looked closer he saw that the beans had sprouted and a beanstalk had grown up overnight. It grew past his window and up towards the sky. It was so tall, the top was hidden in the clouds.

'That old man was right about the beans,' he said to himself. 'They were indeed magic. The beanstalk even looks strong enough to climb.'

The beanstalk had grown close to the cottage, and Jack was able to step onto it straight from his window. Then he started to climb. He climbed until the cottage was a speck below, with the fields spread out all around as far as he could see.

Then he climbed some more until he was in the clouds and could see nothing but fog.

Jack climbed and climbed, higher and higher through the clouds. Just when he thought he could climb no more, he popped out of the cloud and found himself gazing at a beautiful green countryside. A road ran through rolling hills and, in the distance, at the end of the road, stood a castle.

Jack climbed from the beanstalk and set off along the road towards the castle. The closer he got, the bigger the castle seemed to get. When at last he arrived at the front door, he could barely reach the knocker.

The door was opened by the biggest woman he had ever seen.

'What are you doing here?' the woman asked. 'Have you lost your way?'

'No,' said Jack, 'I am just hungry after my long climb.'

'My husband eats little boys. You're lucky I've already made his breakfast, or I'd be tempted to roast you instead.'

'Please don't let your husband eat me,' Jack said. 'But would you spare me a crust of bread and some bacon?'

The woman, although she was a giant, had a kind heart. She invited Jack into the kitchen and gave him some bacon and bread.

'But eat it quickly,' she said. 'My husband will soon be back.'

Suddenly Jack felt the ground shake.

'Quick!' cried the woman. 'Here he comes. Don't let him see you or he will eat you for breakfast.'

The thunderous footsteps came closer and closer. *Thump! Thump! Thump!*

'Hide in the oven,' the woman said. 'You can escape when he has his nap.'

Jack jumped into the oven just in time.

'Fee, fi, fo, fum,' roared the giant.

'I smell the blood of an Englishman.

Be he alive or be he dead

I'll grind his bones to make my bread!'

The giant stomped into the kitchen.

'I smell a juicy little boy!' he bellowed. 'Where is he? Or have you cooked him already, wife?'

'You must be thinking of the boy you ate for dinner last night,' said the woman.

The giant ate his bacon and eggs in great gulps and washed them down with several mugs of tea. When he was finished, he fetched some leather bags from the cupboard and emptied them onto the table. Within moments the tabletop was buried under a mountain of gold coins.

Jack watched through a crack in the oven door as the giant began to count.

The giant was not good at numbers and had to start over several times. Pretty soon he got weary of counting, and before long he dozed off and started to snore.

'Now's my chance,' thought Jack. 'But look at all that gold. Two such coins would keep us fed for a year or more.'

Jack waited until the woman had gone to fetch water from the well, and then he crept out of the oven. Taking care not to disturb the giant, he shovelled as many coins as he could into a bag. Then he heaved it off the table and dragged it all the way back along the road to where the beanstalk poked up through the clouds.

He threw the bag down to earth and scrambled after it down the beanstalk.

At the bottom, he found his mother staring in disbelief at the beanstalk and at the bag of coins that had landed by her feet.

'You see, Mother!' Jack cried. 'I told you those beans were special. Now we no longer have to be poor.'

He told her all about the giant and his wife, and then they went off to market to buy food and everything else they needed. For a time they had plenty to eat and fine things to wear, but eventually they spent all the money and were in danger of being poor again.

Jack knew it was time to climb back up the beanstalk.

So up he went one morning, and once again he arrived at the giant's castle just as the woman was cooking breakfast.

'Good morning, madam,' said Jack, polite as anything. 'I'm hungry from my climb. Can you spare me some of that bread and bacon?'

'You're the same terrible boy who was here the day my husband's gold coins went missing!' she said.

But Jack had grown plump since his last visit, and he was able to talk the giant's wife into believing they had never met.

So, same as last time, she gave him a slab of bacon on toast. She warned him to eat fast because the giant would be home soon, and he would want to eat a boy for breakfast, no doubt about it.

True enough, just as Jack finished eating, the ground began to shake and, quick as a flash, Jack jumped into the oven.

'Fee, fi, fo, fum,' roared the giant.

'I smell the blood of an Englishman.

Be he alive or be he dead

I'll grind his bones to make my bread!'

But his wife quickly slung twenty sausages on the table, and the giant gobbled them down, followed by a bucket of tea.

'Wife,' he bellowed when he was finished, 'bring me my hen!'

The woman scuttled off and fetched a hen whose feathers gleamed with every colour of the rainbow.

'Lay!' the giant commanded.

The hen immediately laid an egg of solid gold.

'Look at that,' thought Jack. 'What Mother and I could do if only we had a hen like this one!'

Just the same as last time, the giant soon grew tired of looking at gold and started to nod off. Before long his snores shook the castle.

Jack slipped out of the oven, grabbed the hen and ran all the way back along the road to the beanstalk.

When he reached home, there was his mother waiting for him.

'What have you got this time?' she asked. 'What use is an old hen?'

'Watch this,' said Jack. He set the hen down and commanded it to lay, which it did. Jack held up the gleaming golden egg, and then told the hen to lay another. 'You see, Mother? We need never be poor again.'

They were indeed never poor again, but living a life of luxury is never as exciting as being poor.

After a while, Jack started to get bored and thought about making another visit to the giant's castle.

So off he went one morning, up the beanstalk and along the road to the giant's castle. But this time, instead of knocking at the front door, Jack crept into the kitchen through the back and found a place to hide in the pantry. He waited for the giant to arrive for his breakfast and before long he heard,

'Fee, fi, fo, fum
I smell the blood of an Englishman.
Be he alive or be he dead
I'll grind his bones to make my bread!'

'If it's that boy who stole your hen,' the woman said, 'I'll help you catch him.'

She went straight to the oven and peered inside. Jack wasn't in the oven, so the giant and his wife searched the castle, high and low. But Jack had hidden deep in a crock in the pantry and they couldn't find him anywhere.

Eventually they gave up and the giant sat down to his breakfast of roast oxen. When he had finished he told his wife to fetch his golden harp.

The harp was made of pure gold, and it sparkled in the sun that streamed through the kitchen windows.

'Sing!' the giant commanded, and the air was instantly filled with exquisite music.

Of course, the giant was soon lulled into a deep sleep, and his snores could be heard for miles around. There was little chance that he would wake—at least, that is what Jack thought.

Once again, he waited for the woman to go out to the well, and then he reached for the harp.

'Help!' the harp cried, as soon as Jack touched it. 'Save me! Master, wake up!'

The giant woke just in time to see Jack run out the door with the harp over his shoulder.

At first the giant thought he was still dreaming, and by the time he realised what had happened, Jack was already gone.

Jack ran and the giant ran after him, and when Jack reached the beanstalk, the giant was close behind.

'The beanstalk will never bear the weight of the giant,' thought Jack.

But the giant wanted his harp back and climbed straight down the beanstalk after Jack.

The beanstalk shuddered and quivered, but it didn't break. And as fast as the giant climbed, Jack climbed faster. And as loud as the harp cried, Jack yelled louder.

'Mother!' he shouted. 'Fetch my axe!'

His mother ran to fetch it, and only just in time. As Jack jumped to the ground with the harp, an enormous pair of feet and legs descended out of the clouds.

Jack chopped furiously at the beanstalk until he chopped it right through. Then the beanstalk came tumbling down, followed by the giant, who fell head first onto the ground.

Now that the giant was dead, the harp obeyed Jack and sang more beautifully than ever. The hen laid golden eggs whenever Jack told it to, and they all lived in luxury for the rest of their lives.

As for the giant's wife, well, who knows?

Little Hare Books
an imprint of
Hardie Grant Egmont
Ground Floor, Building 1, 658 Church Street
Richmond, Victoria 3121, Australia

www.littleharebooks.com

Text copyright © Little Hare Books 2014
Text by Margrete Lamond, with Russell Thomson
Illustrations copyright © Andrew Joyner 2014

First published 2014

Cataloguing-in-Publication details are available from the
National Library of Australia

978 1 742975 24 5 (hbk.)

Designed by Vida & Luke Kelly
Produced by Pica Digital, Singapore
Printed in China by Wai Man Book Binding Ltd.

5 4 3 2 1